ANOTHER LOOK AT THE RAINBOW

AUTHORS

Stephen Bird	13 years	Kurt Miller	13 years
Eric Bottarini	16 years	Coco Nixon	10 years
Tanya Bottarini	9 years	Donald Orr	18 years
Lorrie Bradshaw	6 years	Ed Orr	21 years
Ann Marie Callahan	12 years	Honey Padilla	16 years
Michael Callahan	15 years	Steven Padilla	12 years
Michelle Colson	11 years	Sam Parrish	7 years
Amy Dezendorf	14 years	Carl Radekopf	11 years
Michael Estrada	14 years	Brett Renlund	7 years
Forrest Fennell	10 years	Mariaelena Romero	13 years
Nathaniel Fennell	10 years	Maria Stein	15 years
Paul Harder	12 years	Chet Stevens	14 years
Heather Harris	11 years	Tina Toops	8 years
Deborah Harrison	6 years	Nancy Wilson	10 years
Joanne Hopper	16 years	Krista Woodard	11 years
Kathleen Johansen	20 years	Justin Yungfleish	8 years
Kathy McDonald*	11 years		
Tim McDonald	9 years		

We have listed the ages of the authors as of publication date of this book.
*Cover drawing by.

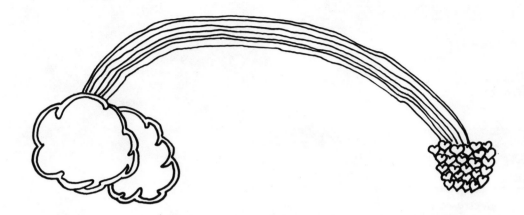

Straight from the Siblings
Another Look at the Rainbow

From the Center for Attitudinal Healing
Edited by Gloria Murray and Gerald G. Jampolsky, M.D.

Celestial Arts
Millbrae, California

First printing, December 1982
Manufactured in the United States of America

Library of Congress Cataloging in Publication Data
Main entry under title:

Another look at the rainbow.

   Summary: A group of thirty-four children share their experiences with terminally ill brothers and sisters.
1. Bereavement in children—Juvenile literature.
2. Brothers and sisters—Juvenile literature.   3. Terminally ill children—Family relationships—Juvenile literature.
(1. Sick—Psychology. 2. Death—Psychological aspects.
3. Brothers and Sisters.   4. Children's writings.)
I. Bird, Stephen.   II. Center for Attitudinal Healing
(Tiburon, Calif.)
BF723.G75A56   1982   155.9′37   82-12951
ISBN 0-89087-341-0 (quality pbk.)

1 2 3 4 5 6 7 8 9 10—88 87 86 85 84 83 82

TO THE PUBLISHER OF THIS BOOK:

When you are deleting, if you do, please be more careful than usual in picking and choosing what will be published. Maybe if you approached the reading as would a child whose brother or sister is catastrophically ill, you would be able to understand the importance and depth of meaning in *every word* chosen by these experienced authors.

Thank you.

Sincerely,
KATHLEEN JOHANSEN

TABLE OF CONTENTS

FOREWORD

The Center for Attitudinal Healing is a free, non-profit educational center that serves as a supplement to the medical model. It is located in Tiburon, California, some twenty miles north of San Francisco.

At the Center we strongly believe that love is the answer to all problems and the most powerful healing force in the world. We define health as inner peace and healing as letting go of fear. One of our basic principles is that as you learn to give help and love to others, your fear disappears and you begin to feel peaceful inside, thus we believe that true happiness comes when you are helping another person.

This is a book written by sisters and brothers of children who have developed an illness from which they may die (a so-called catastrophic illness). The authors of this book began to attend bimonthly meetings at the Center in September, 1976. They wanted to write this book because they thought it would be helpful to other children who might have to face similar problems. They also felt they could help themselves by putting down their thoughts and feelings. The result is this book, which is really notes, from sisters and brothers with love.

The brothers and sisters who have come to our Center have frequently found their lives disrupted and in chaos. They have found it necessary to recognize and feel OK about their experiences of feeling alone, fearful, guilty, resentful and angry. We hope this book will let other siblings know that they are not alone in experiencing these emotions.

The brief introduction at the beginning of each chapter has been written by the co-editors. Otherwise, the words and pictures come from the children who have been part of our sibling group.

It is hoped that the reader will learn that when you let go of the past and future, that when you let this instant be the only time there is . . . an instant only for giving and loving . . . then there will always be hope and the experience of peace.

GLORIA MURRAY
Sibling Facilitator

GERALD G. JAMPOLSKY, M.D.
Consultant

The Center for Attitudinal Healing
Tiburon, California

INTRODUCTION

I think this book had to be written for all kids who find out that their brother or sister is sick with a catastrophic illness. By reading about other people who have had the same thing happen to them, they will understand that they aren't the only people who have these problems, and they may discover how to handle these problems.

When I first discovered my little brother had leukemia there was no book like this around to help me, and so I had to handle these problems by myself.

STEPHEN BIRD
Age 13

ANOTHER LOOK AT THE RAINBOW

1 COMING TOGETHER AS A GROUP

Establishing Trust, Giving Help and Love, Letting Go of Feelings

Brothers and sisters of children who meet at the Center quickly find they are not alone. The group setting provides a safe place for the children to express their thoughts and feelings. This chapter demonstrates how fear disappears when there is a bond of love—and when you are helping each other.

MICHAEL CALLAHAN, age 15
When I first came to the group I was kind of nervous and afraid. I didn't know what to say. . . I just waited for everyone else to talk. As the weeks went by, I felt more comfortable and I began to talk more freely. It helped me get in touch with how I felt. Before that I had a good friend who was a priest and I walked and talked with him when I was upset.

Heather
Harris
age 11

SPEcail Friends are in group

HEATHER HARRIS, age 11

I didn't really talk to anyone before I came to group as I was really shy. It always helps to talk to someone when things are going wrong.

Coming to the group is helpful because when I come I can share my problems with everyone else. Everybody has some sort of problem with a brother or sister. My teacher was nice to me and so was everybody in my class but I couldn't handle things perfectly. In the classroom nobody else has had that sort of experience and no one understood. I have made some special friends in our group.

15

AMY DEZENDORF, age 14

When my mom first mentioned the idea of going to the Center, I didn't want to go. I would only go if there was another nine-year-old girl with a seven-year-old sister with acute lymphoblastic leukemia. I thought that there was nobody else going through what I was going through. But after awhile I realized that there were other people going through this too. I agreed that if someone would get other siblings together that I would come. After a couple of meetings it got easier to talk. I found that I could talk with these people about things I couldn't talk about with my parents. I found out that all of us had a mutual feeling of trust among us. Sometimes I felt lucky that I wasn't having some of the problems that the other people were having. Now we can talk easy to each other. We joke around and talk about previous experiences. I am really glad that I have a place to come to when my sister has problems.

ANN MARIE CALLAHAN, age 12

When we have a problem we can always relate. . .like if you are having trouble in school, or are lonely or scared. You can always talk to your teachers, your family, or your friends here at the Center. You can always phone or write and they will help you with your problem. When you finish you can ask if anybody else needs help. You can keep passing it around because everybody has problems—not always earthshaking problems, but problems.

FORREST FENNELL, age 10

Well, I didn't really know what was going on and I thought I could find out if I came to the group. I never really understood what my sister's sickness was. My mom and dad didn't ever talk to me about it but I knew something was real unhappy. I got to ask things I never asked before.

Sibling's group
can I help?
my sister has problems
I'm worried
What is wrong?
it's O.K. to talk about it
Forrest J.

KRISTA WOODARD, age 11

On August 28th I was at a birthday party for my friend. My mom and brother were at home. . .he was sick so my mom called the ambulance. My grandfather called the party to tell me about him. He was in coma for six hours. I like coming to the group because I can talk about what happened and that helps. We also have outings and fun times together.

JUSTIN YUNGFLEISH, age 8

I was pretty scared at first 'cause I didn't know what was wrong. When your brother has something and you don't know what it is. . .only the name. . .that's pretty scary because you don't know what's going to happen to him.

When I felt sad I would go to my friend's house or school and try to forget about Chad's sickness and my sadness. When I would go to my soccer games, I would forget all about it except when I would kick the ball and then I would think I was kicking the good stuff into his body.

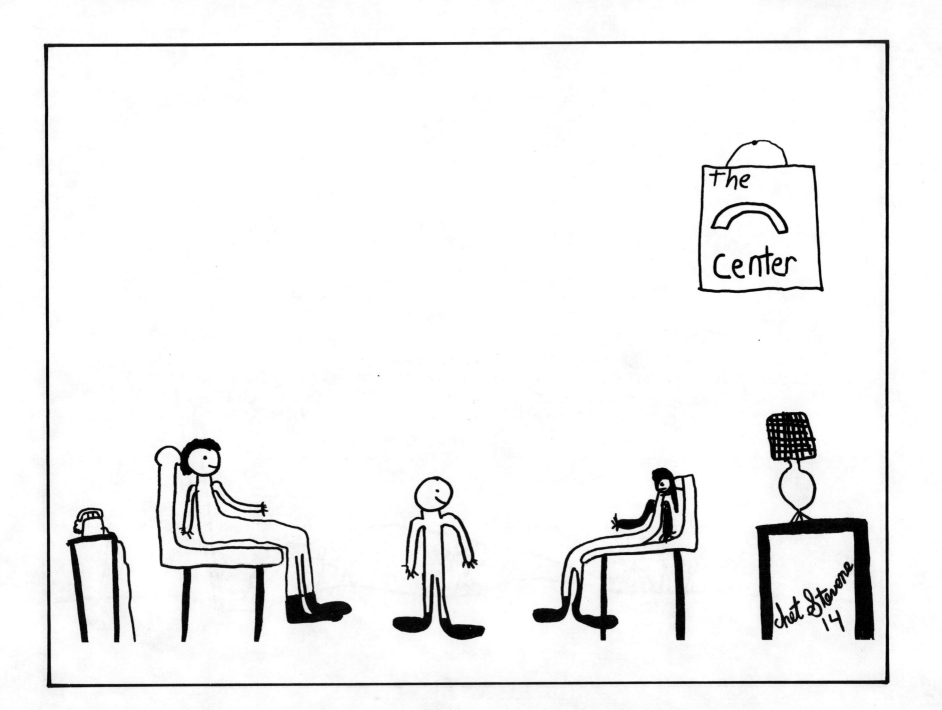

CHET STEVENS, age 14
When I first came to the Center I just thought that it would be a *big* waste of time. But it's not, I found out how "feelings" are with other people and how they deal with them. We talked about how to handle all the pain and frustration their brother or sister was going through. We talked about death too. They taught me to cope with my brother's illness.

NATHANIEL FENNELL, age 10
I liked meeting new friends, and it was fun having pizza. We got to talk about our brothers and sisters and about their sicknesses. That helped me understand why my sister was getting so much attention—but I still didn't like it! I also liked coming along, I didn't like being left at home.

Nathaniel H. Fennell

MARIA STEIN, age 15

I had been afraid to talk about my feelings. I wanted to know if Will might die, but I thought that death was an unspeakable subject. I didn't know how my parents and friends would react to my fears and questions, so I said nothing. My loneliness stopped when we started going to the group meetings. I was thrilled because everyone else had the same feelings, and they were able to talk about them. Whenever I felt really lonely, I knew I could call someone from the group and they could help me with these feelings.

24

ED ORR, age 21

Discussing feelings with people I had never met was hard at first until I realized that we had similar problems and were here to help one another in everyday life. It was helpful coming to the Center and talking about brothers or sisters that we were close to, yet could not play with or see because they were always sick or at the hospital. We all had to deal with parents who were giving more attention and presents to our sick brother or sister, or the fact that he didn't have to go to school while we did and he was playing while we were doing homework. I remember that I really never thought my brother was seriously ill until he lost his hair, got fat, and was nauseated all the time. I didn't know what to do, I was fearful of his dying, until I went to the Center and my new friends helped me.

JUSTIN YUNGFLEISH, age 8
When I come to the Center I go upstairs to our group. First we eat together and then we have a circle to give love to people who are sick. We have a big picture with everyone's handprints on it. The picture I drew was for my brother. It was two good cells holding hands under a rainbow.

2 OUR FIRST REACTIONS

In this chapter the authors share what their first reaction was to their brothers' and sisters' illnesses. They talk about their fears of the possibility that the illness may result in death.

STEPHEN BIRD, age 13

When I first found out that my little brother was sick, I thought it was just a cold. One day when my relatives from Canada came over, he didn't feel good at all so we took him to the hospital.

The next day my dad came home and I asked why he spent the night at the hospital. He told me that Jim had leukemia, and I thought it was a funny word for the flu.

About a week later I found out what leukemia really was and I felt very sad. I wondered why I didn't get it. I ran up on a hill and I sat there throwing rocks. That really took the anger out of me and now, whenever I get mad, I go and climb up there.

by Steve Bird
age 13

age 11
Kurt Miller

HEATHER HARRIS, age 11

I was only six years old and my younger sister had a stroke and her kidneys failed. I found out by listening to my parents' conversations because I was afraid to ask what had happened to her. I was fairly scared. . . . I cried a lot after that. I was worried and I kept my feelings to myself. . . . My stomach was always in a knot. I tried to take life one day at a time but it really hurt. I had to learn a lot of things on my own. When I was upset I said to myself, "You've got to figure out what to do to stop this pain. . ."

KURT MILLER, age 13

My mom took me back in a room and told me that my brother, Keith, had cancer and he might die. I asked her where did it come from. She said if they had known they might have been able to stop it.

I asked her why did he get it and not someone else. And then I started to cry and I felt like dying.

TANYA BOTTARINI, age 9
One day Tony had cancer and I did not know that he had cancer. When I found out what cancer was, I thought Tony was going to die. But my mom told me he wasn't going to die. Then I wasn't afraid any more. Then Tony went to the hospital. Tony had bad cells that could kill him, so the doctors had to take his leg off. After he had his leg amputated he had a fake leg. Tony had chemotherapy to help him kill the bad cells of his body.

ERIC BOTTARINI, age 16
I was scared, but I knew he could pull through it—no matter what was happening to him.

MARIA STEIN, age 15
When I first heard that Will might have cancer, I was a little bit scared, excited, but it didn't really bug me. The thought never occurred to me then that Will might die.

CHET STEVENS, age 14

Why was his hair falling out? Why was he going to the hospital all the time? Why was he getting bone marrows all the time? It never occurred to me that he might die. What was happening? I didn't get to go to the hospital to see him. What was leukemia? Why was he getting so many presents???

AMY DEZENDORF, age 14

Well, here I am. Wondering what I am doing, why I am sitting here on the sixth floor of the hospital. Afraid and scared about what is going on. All they have told me is that my little sister is very sick and has some sort of disease.

After a few minutes I went into a conference room. In there were my parents, the doctor and my sister. My little sister was looking so different. She looked skinny and pale. Oh what a change from my bright and happy sister! My mother looked weepy and my father, upset. My sister had leukemia, a form of cancer that is life-threatening. My sister might die. The thought came to me like a punch in the stomach. I finally caught on. It was so scarey! Why did my sister get this? Why not me? I was so confused inside I didn't know what to do, so I cried.

STEVEN PADILLA, age 12

The first time I heard that my brother was sick I started to cry. Because we were so close I worried about him night and day, during school and at dinner. During school I couldn't work. My friends and his friends felt sorry for us. It was sad to think about him the way he was.

JOANNE HOPPER, age 16

My sister, Jeana, is 12 years old. She has a physical handicap. She wasn't born with this. When she was three years old she contracted strep throat; the illness went to her kidneys, and she had a cardiac arrest. The lack of oxygen to her brain caused brain damage, which affected her vision and her physical mobility.

When she was in the hospital I was about six. I was sheltered from all this. My mother didn't tell me what was going on because she wanted to protect my feelings. I was so angry because Jeana and I were so close. Our parents are divorced and Mom had to work, but we always had each other. I was so terribly afraid. I didn't know what was happening; I was afraid of the unknown. If you know what the problem is, you can face up to it and work it out; but if you don't understand, you can't handle it.

When I finally found out what happened, it was so hard to talk about it especially when someone says, "Hey, what's wrong with your sister? Why is she in a wheel chair?" People can be such jerks sometimes! They just don't understand!!

It really bothers me when someone calls Jeana "crippled." It sounds so terrible. Even handicapped seems so sickly; I prefer to say that Jeana is "physically challenged."

I blamed myself. I constantly felt guilty around her. I wanted to punish myself somehow. "Why me!!" Why couldn't it happen to a murderer or someone who is out there hurting other people?

It helped when I had to explain about Jeana's illness in group. We always had new people coming in and the first time I had to share it was really frightening. I knew inside it wasn't my fault but I was so hurt, lost, and mixed up that I blamed myself. Having to say it over made me face up to it more and not feel so ashamed.

3 WHAT IS GOING ON?

In general, our children are curious and want to know as many details as possible about what is going on with their sibling. They want to know as much as their parents about the disease, what the medicines do, what the side effects are, and what they can do to help. They are concerned about being left out, particularly when they are not allowed to visit the hospital.

What was going on in your heart and in your mind after your first reaction?

KURT MILLER, age 13
I wanted to know if Keith was going to die or not. I wondered what the doctors and nurses did to him in the hospital. I wish the doctor had told me his hair would fall out. It surprised me when I saw him bald. It would scare me when he was throwing up because I thought he was dying. Later on I found out that his baldness and his throwing up were side effects of medicine.

Kurt Miller
age 11

Sometimes you wonder what kind of medicine your brother or sister is getting and what kind of doctors are making it.

My advice to others is to try to get as much information as you can. I was one of the last ones in my neighborhood to find out he had cancer.

MIKE ESTRADA, age 14

I was curious to know what the disease was. I was wondering if it was going to be the end of my brother or not. I asked myself, *why not me?* I was just wondering why it was happening to my family, why it wasn't happening to some other family. I am sure glad he is still alive.

DON ORR, age 18

It was hard. They were telling me stuff that I really didn't understand. At that time he and I were really close. He was getting sick and we couldn't do much. I was wondering why he couldn't do things any more. And if I got in an argument and hit him, I was always afraid my hit would cause him to die. I felt lonely not having a little brother to play with or beat up.

MARIA STEIN, age 15

After William's operation to see whether the tumor was malignant or not (I didn't know what malignant meant then), he was crabby, but I didn't get mad at him because I felt *sorry* for him. He had to spend his birthday in the hospital. Luckily he got to spend Christmas at home.

ERIC BOTTARINI, age 16

When my brother had his leg amputated, I wondered if he would ever be able to skateboard or ride a bike again.

Then the first day out of the hospital he rode a skateboard. Now he can ride a bike, a horse, and do anything. My brother Tony's ability to deal with the problem helped me to have the strength to deal with it too.

NANCY WILSON, age 10

I wanted to know why Allan had to go to the hospital.

I wonder what they're doing in there ???

Nancy Wilson

What were your reactions to your brother or sister's hair falling out and to some other things that were happening?

CARL RADEKOPF, age 11
I felt very embarrassed. . .

KRISTA WOODARD, age 11
My hospital was good, I got to help with the radiation machine. I'd have to get out real quick. I didn't like it when Jamal threw up all over the car. Jamal had a seizure and all the neighbors knew because the ambulance came.

MARIA STEIN, age 15

William's hair came out so gradually that I didn't really notice. But other people did, especially my friends. On my birthday I had some friends spend the night. In the morning William was eating breakfast with us. I noticed all my friends were quiet, which was unusual for them. When we went downstairs after breakfast to get dressed, they all started swarming around me, asking questions. "What happened to your brother?" Or, "Why is your brother bald?" I realized that none of my friends had been prepared, so it must have been quite a shock. It would probably be a good idea to let people know what they're in for. I feared that William would die, and because all my brothers and sisters had moved, I would be like an *only child*.

My advice is that doctors and parents ought to give information to the *brothers and sisters straight!* Sometimes, instead of telling them the truth, parents and doctors tell siblings a lot of baloney. It is easier to handle when you at least have all the facts.

SAM PARRISH, age 7

Isaac was almost bald. He needed a hair net 'cause it got all over him and made him itch.

SAM-BATTRELL-PARRISH
AGE 7½

43

4
FEAR, LONELINESS, JEALOUSY AND GUILT

All of our children at one time or another feel fear, loneliness, guilt and jealousy. And when experiencing these emotions they seem to feel a lack of love—both from within and from without.

As our children begin to share their most painful and fearful feelings with others and find them to be totally acceptable, they begin to let go of them. As they learn to help and give love to each other, they find these feelings simply vanish. They discover the power of unconditional love, and that giving and receiving are one and the same.

PAUL HARDER, age 12
When I first grew up I wondered why one of my sisters had a disease. I wondered why I didn't get it. I just guessed that some people were lucky. Maybe God wanted some people to be crippled and some He didn't or maybe He thought that the world would be too crowded for everyone, but I thought that wasn't the reason because everyone dies.

AMY DEZENDORF, age 14

I knew that I would rather be healthy with less attention than be sick with cancer and get a lot of attention.

I was green with envy at first. My sister was just lying in bed and receiving all of this merchandise: nightgowns, sheets, stuffed animals and books. Will it ever end?

Then I took a second away from envy. Hey, I thought. What am I jealous of? Here I am healthy and standing upright; my sister was lying in bed with her life being threatened. These presents were not going to help her sickness any. Then I started to feel sorry for her!

I was so confused!

KURT MILLER, age 13
Getting lots of things isn't really going to cure the cancer. It is just going to make him feel better. He might be getting lots of toys but you're not the one getting chemotherapy and you don't have the disease.

FORREST FENNELL, age 10

I mostly missed my mom a lot. She was always away at the hospital with my sister. My brother and I had to stay with Mom's friends or our neighbors all day. When my sister came home and she was mean or bad, she got away with it. If I hit her I got spanked. Why was she so special?

NATHANIEL FENNELL, age 10

When my sister was in the hospital with leukemia my mother gave all her attention to her and she was hardly ever home. And my sister got extra presents. I almost wished I could be sick, too.

JOANNE HOPPER, age 16

I have always been jealous about the attention Jeana receives for Jeana has been handicapped for almost ten years. I've pretty much learned to live with it. It's now just a part of my life that I'm left out sometimes. Everyone doesn't mean to leave me out but I'm not going to sit around and feel sorry for myself.

My sister always takes medicine to control her seizures, but sometimes we try to take her off the medication and she usually faints or is really tired. She's never had a violent seizure, thank God! My friend's mother has epilepsy and she sometimes has a seizure, when this happens it's emotionally stressful for the whole family. It makes me hurt inside.

I'm afraid mostly for Jeana. She's blind so she can't drive and the buses aren't safe. There's no way she can defend herself if someone should attack her. And what's she going to do for a career? She's intelligent but she cannot use her hands very well. Jeana is a very hard worker and she's very determined. Maybe an employer will recognize her good qualities and accept the things she can't do.

MARIAELENA ROMERO, age 13

The first time my brother got sick all anyone would ask was, "How is Randy?" I didn't mind that but, because I wasn't 12, I couldn't go into my brother's hospital room. I am the littlest one so I got jealous; I said I understood, but I didn't. The second time I understood.

When I visited Randy in the hospital he would complain about my nervous habits. I didn't always like to see him because he blames me for everything. Because I am so much younger and smaller when I was angry at my brother I couldn't hit him because he could hit me back harder.

CHET STEVENS, age 14

Jealousy is envy! Most all of us are envious of someone who gets all the attention. Sometimes it's hard for us to know why our brother or sister gets more attention than we do. Many times we think we are getting ripped off when we are actually the lucky ones.

AMY DEZENDORF, age 14

"How is Andrea, your sister, doing today? Is she home from the hospital yet? Will she get better soon? Send her my love."

When your brother or sister is sick, this is what you might hear. This is all I heard for about a year after Andrea was sick. I was so sick of hearing all of this stuff about Andrea I could scream. Why doesn't anyone ever ask *me* how I am doing!!! Andrea was not allowed to see anyone, and none of my friends could come over. How come no one could come over? I wish I had someone to talk to.

ERIC BOTTARINI, age 16

My brother has to suffer because he is always in the hospital and not out playing in the fields with me and my friends having a ball of a time and he was not there to play with us.

He has to take all this medicine to help digest his food and nothing he drinks or eats tastes good to him. He has a lot of medicine to take all day and it must get boring for him. It is painful to go to the hospital and get a lot of shots. And those needles don't feel exactly too good in the leg or arm. Sometimes he does not feel good when he gets out of the hospital so we leave him alone to sleep the pain off and relax in a warm bed in peace and quiet. At the hospital nowadays it is noisy and anything but peaceful. There is no time to think of home or pleasure or relaxation.

MARIA STEIN, age 15

I had a hard time accepting William's grouchiness, but after awhile I realized that it was the drugs, and not me, that were making Will so uncomfortable. After that his moods didn't bother me so much. I finally realized that there was no reason to be jealous because everyone gave William more attention because he needed it, not because they like him better than me.

HONEY PADILLA, age 16

I felt I had to hold my feelings in when I was around my parents. I let my feelings out only when I was with my close friends.

HEATHER HARRIS, age 11

My sister's seizures are getting much worse lately. I am really frightened. I stay in my room and my parents take care of her, there is nothing I can do to help. It is kind of scary to talk to my friends about her, but I would rather have them ask me than stare.

MIKE ESTRADA, age 14

When your brother or sister becomes sick they get all the attention. The reason why is your brother or sister might not have much time to live. So your parents are doing the best for them.

TINA TOOPS, age 8

I worry all the time when my brother is going to have to stay in the hospital. I can't go into his room because I'm under 12 years old. But he can come out of his room. When I went to the hospital I saw a lot of people who were sick. I wasn't very happy. Mom and Dad were not happy either. I went into the waiting room and watched TV. Mom and Dad took turns going into my brother's room. When I was little I used to think that my brother was going to die. He wouldn't take the medicine and he would throw up afterwards. I missed my parents a lot 'cause I had to stay with my aunt and friends all the time.

On November 15th, 1981 my brother went to the hospital again, this time for a kidney transplant from Dad. I was scared that it wouldn't work. I was dreaming about what it would be like if my brother went to heaven. It seemed weird in our house because I'm so used to having four people at the table and there were only two. I'm not worried now because I think it's going to work out OK.

55

MARIA STEIN, age 15

Why, why, why was the question I asked myself so many times when my brother, William, was sick. I also asked God, but it seemed like there never was a good answer. It was so hard to see Will in a great deal of pain and trying not to complain or cry.

It made me depressed and many times I would run into my room and pray for Will to be out of pain and then I would break down and cry. Many times it wouldn't work but it was very gratifying when I would hear William drift off into a peaceful sleep. I am having a hard time since my brother died. It's very lonely without him but it's good to know that he's not in pain anymore.

5
FACING
THE PROBLEM
OF
DEATH

One of the worst problems that faces all of us is our conscious or unconscious fear of death. Many of us go through life without facing directly what our true thoughts are about life and death, who we really are and what our purpose is here on earth.

In this chapter the brothers and sisters express their most intimate feelings with candor, love and sensitivity.

STEVEN BIRD, age 13
On August 15th, 1980 my little brother died of a stroke. He had a blood clot in his neck because of too much radiation. His death was a real shock to me and I was very scared. I was afraid of what the rest of my life would be like without him. As time moved on, the thought of his death wasn't so bad anymore because I started to live my life. I started to feel better.

I think the best way is to get your mind off of it. I was invited to go fishing. I had a good time. When I came home I felt upset again but I realized that when I had a fun time I didn't feel sad.

KATHLEEN JOHANSEN, age 20

Talking with other children whose brother or sisters have died helps a lot in getting me out of my depression or "pity party," as my brother used to say. When I can listen to, be with, or share with another person, we both feel better and, through the sharing, it's amazing how fast and deep a friendship can be developed.

Before my brother died, whenever I got depressed I would go into his room and hold his hand. He couldn't talk or hear but holding his hand straightened me out. It made me realize that all I wanted was to be with him and make him happy.

Now, certain songs, the color blue, toy soldiers, and seeing mail that comes for him, or other boys his age playing make me think of him. Often I get very lonely but then I think, "It was great having Paul as a brother."

I am happier having had the special relationship with my brother for a short amount of time than I would be having a brother grow up and not having a special friendship.

KATHY McDONALD, age 11

When we first learned my brother was sick we were told that he could die. We all felt that he could recover. Other people died but *not Billy.* Why Billy? Why not someone else? When Billy told me he was going to die I didn't believe him (though I had come to believe that he might). I thought it was one of his silly jokes.

While walking home from school, Dad met me and he said, "Billy's better than ever and he won't suffer any more." Then I said, "How is he, is he all right?" *"He has died,"* said Dad. So I walked up to the house not knowing what to expect and how our lives would change, wondering if we could ever be happy that Christmas.

Our house was filled with close family and friends. Jerry was there also. The mood was bad. I felt the support of those special people. I knew my Mom and Dad were hurting.

We still had our chores to do, feeding the farm animals. Giving Bluey, our family dog, extra love, knowing she is missing Billy.

Billy's funeral mass was the Mass of the Angels. Heaven is Billy's new home now. It has been two years since Billy died. Memories of him are fading. Although at times I will remember things we did together. His memory occupies a special place in my heart. At times I feel he pulls strings for me. Heaven to me is the place you go to when you die and heaven is anything you want it to be. For Billy, it is riding his horse, Patches, and being happy.

61

MARIA STEIN, age 15

There are several ways to look at death. One is to see it not as the end of everything but a stage of life ending, with others to come. Another is to think that your brother or sister will not have any more pain, it will be a release for them. We will miss them, but we still want the best for our loved ones. However you look at it, the reason we fear death is because we don't know what it is. If you can come to terms with it in your own mind, decide what we think it really is, it will lessen the fear of death.

I talked to many people. People in our group, friends and my parents and asked them what they thought about death. I then turned it over in my own mind until it made enough sense to me so that I felt more comfortable about the thought of death.

Whatever you do, *don't hold your feelings in.* Whatever they are, get them out before they harm you. If you feel like crying, then cry. If you don't let go of your feelings, they build up until you're about to have a nervous breakdown. . .*really!!!!!*

STEVEN PADILLA, age 12

This is a picture of me and my brother playing baseball. I didn't draw my brother on the pitcher's mound where he usually was. . . .I made first-string catcher and he made first-string pitcher. Now I play center field.

Wish He Would Have Never Had Left Me!!!

DEBORAH HARRISON, age 6

My little brother Aric was four-and-one-half years old. He had a brain tumor, he had to go to the hospital. After awhile he couldn't see and then we helped him to learn where things were in our house.

I didn't like having no attention at all even when Mommy and Daddy were home. I went to Nancy's house 'cause I couldn't stand the screaming and crying.

This is a picture of my little brother Aric's service. We held hands way up on a hill in Armstrong Woods. We were quiet and closed our eyes and we thought of Aric. Then we started singing the Rainbow Connection. But we all knew Aric was safe and happy up in heaven. Then I ran in the hills with my friends Lucas, Emily and Andre.

We didn't like having Aric dead because we were all friends. We were sad.

This picture is of a man in the real old days before most of the people were born and he is standing on top of my brother Aric's grave. He is saying "Let there be Peace!!" But Aric made two flowers grow around his grave. So we knew he was *so* happy up there in heaven.

Many of you have mentioned heaven. What do you think it is like?

CHET STEVENS, age 14
I think it is a place where there is peace.

MARIAELENA ROMERO, age 13
My idea of heaven is that it will be real clean and white and cloudy.

BRETT RENDLUND, age 7
I drew a picture of Eric in heaven. Daddy and I are singing and Eric is going to the angels and the light.

When You are in Heaven, You are not sick anymore.
You have wings on. You are happy and LOVE
And God is talking to you.

BYran

age 5

6
Lonnie

KATHLEEN JOHANSEN, age 20

My ideas about what heaven is have come a complete circle. When I was little I thought my grandparents and everyone I lost would be up there in bodies. But as I grew older I realized, as everyone does, that it wouldn't be the same; that in heaven we would not be reunited as we were on earth but in another dimension which cannot be defined. But ever since my brother died I keep thinking we'll be back together again as we were here because that was heaven.

Yet through my brother's death, and my questions about life after, I've had a constant debate between my logical self,—that realizes that the ideas of my younger days are impossible,—and my heart, or my "wishful self"—that longs for the security of my earlier dreams about heaven and a reunion with my brother and myself as we were.

HEAVEN

TINA TOOPS, age 8

I think that when you first die, if you have not said your prayers you go to this place that starts with a *P*. . .you can't get out by yourself. If you pray every night he'll finally let you out. Heaven has gates and people with wings (maybe that's a fairytale), and I can see my relatives, Uncle Johnnie and Great Great Grandma, and my brother's hamster there.

HEATHER HARRIS, age 11

I think that when you die you are happier because you are not suffering anymore. Even the little inconveniences are gone. Treatment is gone for those who needed it. Hopefully we go up to heaven (the perfect place) and have nothing to worry about. You'll see all your relatives that have died, even the dogs, cats and hamsters that have died too. My picture shows me with my pass to the gate to heaven. My pets, relatives and friends are waiting for me behind the gate.

6
MAKING LIFE AN UPPER... YOU HAVE A CHOICE

At the Center, we believe that we don't have to act like robots. We have a choice about what we think. And we can decide to have happy thoughts or sad thoughts.

In this chapter brothers and sisters who have gone through the pain of having their siblings seriously ill offer helpful suggestions for others who may be facing a family crisis.

Knowing that you had a choice to be sad or happy, what did you do that helped?

HEATHER HARRIS, age 11
I learned you didn't have to hold everything in. . .it was OK to cry. I like to do quiet things like play with paper dolls and read to help me think of other things. If I talk to somebody it usually solves almost all of my problems. I would tell a new child in the group about my experience and that the group works, that it teaches them how to let go of their pain—the sadness about what has happened—and that the pain will not be permanent.

MARIAELENA ROMERO, age 13
I go in my room and do what I want or try to think of something else. I listen to the radio, watch TV or read a book. I try to get my mind off my worries. IT WORKS!!! But they come back and you have to keep trying to think of something else.

HONEY PADILLA, age 16
My advice to others is that when you are lonely, keep busy and don't give up hope.

KURT MILLER, age 13
I talked to my brother, Keith, as if nothing was happening and it made him feel better.

   I prayed. I got my mind on other things and just felt positive that everything was going to go good.

DEBORAH HARRISON, age 6
I try not to think about it. . .

DON ORR, age 18
My advice to others is don't feel left out. The hardest part was having the guilt. I'd advise others not to feel guilty if you get angry at your brother.

TINA TOOPS, age 8
Some things that you can do to make yourself not worry are: You can talk about it, or you can roller skate or go hiking and forget about it for awhile. You can pray and give thanks for your blessings and share your love. I prayed the *Hail Mary* and *Our Father* and a prayer of my own. It goes like this. . .

> Love is sweet
> Love is nice
> Love is kind
> And always sharing

And that made me feel better.

MICHELLE COLSON, age 11
When I was feeling sad and depressed I went and talked to my
dog, Tahoe, and that really made me feel better.

MARIA STEIN, age 15

We moved to Houston and no one knew my brother had died. It was nice getting a fresh start. It was my choice if I wanted to tell somebody.

Sometimes in my old school when I would get bored in class, I would get very depressed and cry. I was stuck in a rut and I needed to do it all again, to start from the beginning.

I decided I can be depressed or I can do something about it. It brings other people down when I'm down. I decided I'd rather be in a good mood so I changed my attitude.

Now when I'm in school and bored and my mind wanders and I get depressed, I try to think about upcoming events that will brighten my day. I talk to my friends and they help me a lot. They always tease me and show me how to look on the bright side of things.

It's hard to make it through the day but knowing that right after school I can go to the drama department and sing and dance my frustrations away helps.

It has been fantastic here. I have become more mature, especially when it comes to death or sick people. I can support them now. I appreciate the world a lot more.

KATHLEEN JOHANSEN, age 20

When I am really depressed I crawl into bed with my Teddy Bear. . .believe it or not!!!

Or when I am really into myself I'll pork out on pizza or mint chocolate chip ice cream with the destined result of an increase in my weight, and then I feel even more depressed.

It has helped me to play side one of Boston's first album, especially the song, *Peace of Mind,* which was one of my brother's favorite songs. Or listen to the Blues Brothers album to remind myself of the joy my brother and I both got out of clowning around to those songs.

What really picks me up is to take a bike ride. Bike rides when I am depressed help expend the energy that I have because of the stored-up anger inside of me. When I return to my room, I feel more relaxed and peaceful and again can believe that I am glad my brother is out of pain and that I am personally stronger as a result of the cancer experience.

KATHY McDONALD, age 11

When I feel sad I usually go to my horse and talk to him or go to our puppy who makes everything happy. The antics of my goat would cheer up anyone's sadness. There are many other things you can do to help.

When Billy was sick we all worked together on an imagery for him that was sung to his favorite jazzy tune. He had an incredible sense of humor and that helps a lot. The words went something like this:

> Imagery, imagery
> Everybody gots imagery
> You can use it when you're getting a shot
> Or you can use it when you're hot.

After Billy died my brother, Tim, and I wanted to buy him a birthday present. Mom suggested flowers but the funeral had so many flowers we didn't like that suggestion. We learned from the radio that there is an adoption program for animals at the San Francisco Zoo. So we put in fifteen dollars and adopted a giraffe because Billy had a favorite stuffed giraffe. We have planted daffodils for him and named a star for him also.

We are still a family. Billy is just somewhere else. And that somewhere else is heaven.

I still love you,
Billy

Tim age 9

7
THOUGHTS FOR OTHERS ON GOING ON THROUGH LIFE

The following are comments—based on the authors' experiences— that they thought would be helpful to other siblings.

TANYA BOTTARINI, age 9
Take one day at a time.

ERIC BOTTARINI, age 16
Take life as it comes to you. Be aware of what is going on and find someone to help.

KATHLEEN JOHANSEN, age 20
Don't think about yourself. Become a better listener and think about others. What helps me is a saying I have hanging in my room: "If you see someone without a smile, give them yours."

FORREST FENNELL, age 10
Don't be afraid to cry, don't be afraid to show your feelings.

NATHANIEL FENNELL, age 10
Try to joke and look at things differently.

KRISTA WOODARD, age 11
If you are sad or upset, read a book to get your mind off the problem. Having a friend sure helps a lot.

DON ORR, age 18
Don't feel sorry for yourself. If your parents are not paying attention to you, remind yourself and know that they still love you. It is just that they have to pay more attention to the person who is sick.

KURT MILLER, age 13
When you are upset, you need to learn when to be alone to work it out and when it is best to be with your friends.

MICHELLE COLSON, age 11
If you have questions, don't be afraid to ask them. Remind yourself that if your brother or sister dies that heaven is a nice place.

CARL RADEKOPF, age 11
Forget about the problems of the past. . .and decide to live a happy life.

COCO NIXON, age 10
It always works for me when I am upset to ride my bike and to keep busy. If you are sad. . .find a friend to play with and get your mind off your troubles.

8
SUMMARY: STRAIGHT FROM THE SIBLINGS

Learning ways of overcoming death from children can be one of the most beautiful, powerful learning experiences in the world.

AMY DEZENDORF, age 14
We all learned different things and we all had our own ways to deal with this problem. I learned to value the days. . .just one at a time, to take them as they came. I learned to keep on the bright side. The problem is unavoidable and it helps to talk about it. It changed my life in a positive way. It made me feel lucky that it didn't happen to me. Remember with the bad things the good things come too!!!!!

DON ORR, age 18
Don't think about death. . .Just think about life and think only about the positive side of things.

KURT MILLER, age 13

I only thought grownups got cancer. I was more *scared* than surprised when my brother had cancer. I thought you just died when you got cancer. At the Center I learned that death is possible to overcome. I stopped being scared by thinking positively and praying.

MICHAEL CALLAHAN, age 15

I learned to talk about my sister's problem and how it affected me. For me, talking about it instead of just *thinking* about it was helpful. Talking together in a group helped all of us to cope with the problem of our families. I feel my sister's illness made us closer as a family. We were all in it "together." When she was very ill we prayed every night with our grandmother for her recovery. I wanted to see her well again. Pray and do whatever you can to help the family and whoever is sick.

STEVEN BIRD, age 13

I heard about death but it seemed far off and I never thought it would happen to someone in our family.

When a brother or sister becomes seriously ill, it's hard to accept, and it makes you look at life differently. It was rough and I had to learn that someone close to me could die and that I would never see him again.

It made me think about my own death and to learn to live day by day. Now I don't think that death is the end of life. . .it is just moving on to another stage of life.

ED ORR, age 21

The whole experience of meeting with other siblings made me not think of my brother, Joey, as having a disease. I learned from my brother a lot about life. I no longer take life for granted and I make the most out of each minute. I learned *that* from Joey and the other siblings. Since Joey has been sick, I have had a lifetime goal of helping children with everyday problems. That's why I am going to school now and studying special education.

KATHLEEN JOHANSEN, age 20
When we love someone we can feel that love forever, whether the person is with us in body or not.

MARIA STEIN, age 14
I've learned to live each day as if it were the last and I try to live each day to the fullest. I try to resolve things each night before I go to bed. Everyone needs emotional support and the best person to give you that support is another kid who is going through the same thing. The group was like having a big family where you could share everything. . .no matter what it was. Helping each other at the Center helped me get rid of fear.

I've learned that I help myself when I help others. So now I volunteer at a hospital. I find that when I concentrate on loving and helping another person, I can forget my problem and my own depression. With love you can make it through anything.

What Makes Me Smile

The sun,
Stretching its rosy fingers over the horizon,
It's golden glow like a smile made in heaven.

A child's laughter,
Falling on my ears like a bird's song,
Sweeter than the tinkling of bells.

The thrill of victory,
Coursing through my body,
Making me feel invincible.

Falling rain,
Forming sparkling patterns on my window,
Its soothing rhythm accompanying my thoughts.

A finished book,
Its secrets now revealed,
Fulfilling the need of a curious mind.

A friendly smile,
From across a crowded room,
Melting my loneliness into a dream.

Most of all,
The goal reached, the promise fulfilled,
Brings a joyous smile to my face.

—by Maria Stein

EPILOGUE

Gloria Murray, co-editor of this book, helped found the Sibling Group in 1976 and served as its facilitator until the fall of 1981. Gloria is now serving our Center in another capacity and it was felt that her comments would make a suitable epilogue.

GLORIA MURRAY

I am very grateful to have had the opportunity to work with these young people. For through the years they have taught me about the marvelous resiliency of spirit.

I have an overwhelming sense of the deep love felt between brothers and sisters. It's a very powerful connection that overcomes the more frequently expressed sibling rivalry and forms an unbreakable bond.